To Coral Elizabeth.
Seek what is good, beautiful, and true.

Many thanks to the Northeast
community group kiddos, especially Sofia.

Published in 2021 by Beaming Books, an imprint of 1517 Media. All rights reserved.
No part of this book may be reproduced without the written permission of the publisher.
Email copyright@1517.media. Printed in [country name here.]

27 26 25 24 23 22 21   1 2 3 4 5 6 7 8

Hardcover ISBN: 978-1-5064-6379-7
Ebook ISBN: 978-1-5064-6652-1

Library of Congress Cataloging-in-Publication Data

Names: Shipman, Talitha, author, illustrator.
Title: Finding beauty / by Talitha Shipman.
Description: Minneapolis, MN : Beaming Books, 2021. | Audience: Ages 3-8. |
    Summary: Illustrations and easy-to-read text reveal that if one looks,
    one can find beauty in objects big and small, alone or with a friend,
    and that beauty will find those who look for it.
Identifiers: LCCN 2019056846 (print) | LCCN 2019056847 (ebook) | ISBN
    9781506463797 (hardcover) | ISBN 9781506466521 (ebook)
Subjects: CYAC: Aesthetics--Fiction. | Conduct of life--Fiction.
Classification: LCC PZ7.1.S517713 Fin 2021 (print) | LCC PZ7.1.S517713
    (ebook) | DDC [E]--dc23
LC record available at https://lccn.loc.gov/2019056846
LC ebook record available at https://lccn.loc.gov/2019056847

CPSIA: VN0004589; 9781506463797; DEC2020

Beaming Books
510 Marquette Avenue
Minneapolis, MN 55402

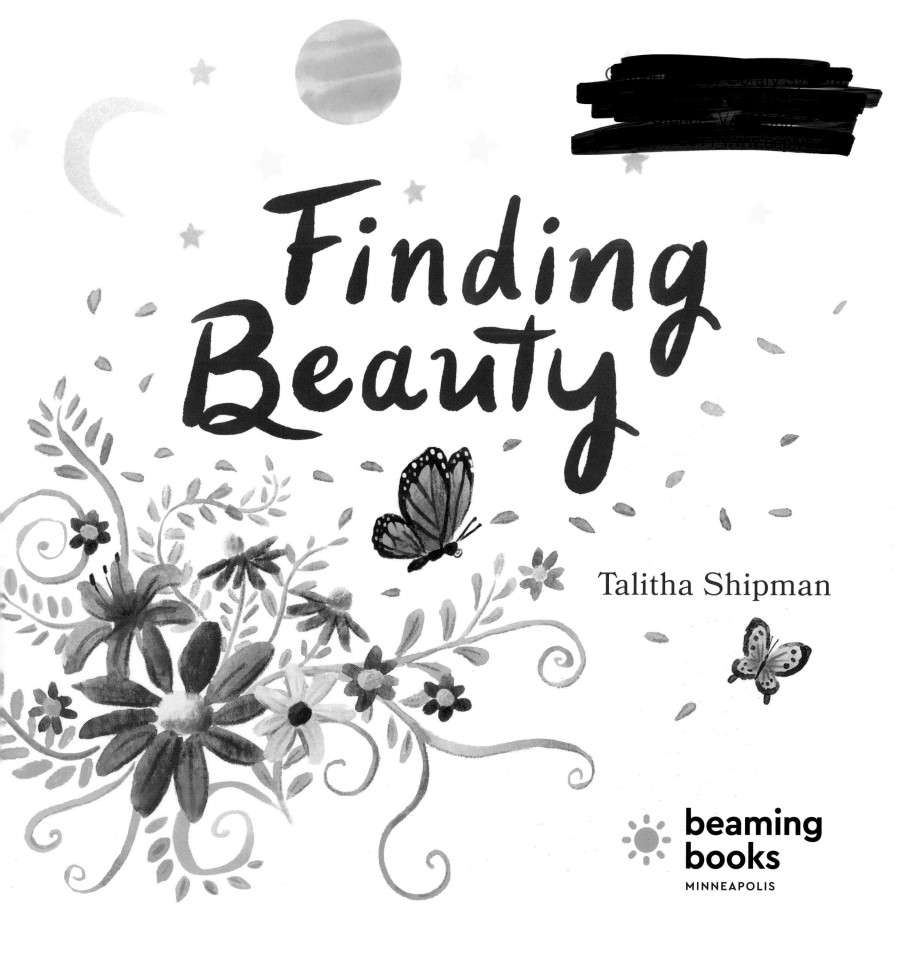

Finding Beauty

Talitha Shipman

beaming
books
MINNEAPOLIS

When you were a baby, everyone said,
"What a beautiful girl!"

They saw your sweet little face,
your button nose.

You were perfect,
from the top of your head
to the tips of your toes.

But there's a secret not everyone knows.

Beauty surrounds you if you look for it,

in things big

and small.

You might find beauty by yourself,

or with a friend.

X

b

center

diameter

radii

Z

P

Y

You can find beauty in numbers

X = ___ cm

Golden
Spiral

34

21

13

Nautilus Shell

Fibona
Sequ

$\frac{1}{2} = 1 \times 0.5 = 0.5$

perpendicular

and in stars too many to count

And then one day,
because you have been looking,
beauty will find you!

It will be in everyone you meet.

It will waft from windows

and peek around corners.

Beauty may whisper a poem,
sing a song, paint a picture.

Beauty will call from broken things too.

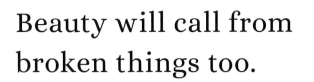

And when you are sad,
beauty will fly to you.

In spring flowers,
summer storms,
falling leaves,
and sparkling snow,

and from the top of your head
to the tips of your toes,
you will find beauty,
wherever you go.

ABOUT THE AUTHOR

 **TALITHA SHIPMAN** lives in Fort Wayne, Indiana, with her husband and their three-year-old wild child, Coral. Her favorite subjects to paint are wild kids and wild animals. Nature inspires Talitha's painting, and she hopes her work encourages curiosity and creativity in children of all ages. Talitha has worked with publishers large and small. Her books include the Sidney Taylor Honor recipient *Everybody Says Shalom* by Leslie Kimmelman (Random House Books for Young Readers, 2015); an American Farm Bureau Recommended Read, *Applesauce Day* by Lisa Amstutz (Albert Whitman, 2017); a 2019 IPPY Silver Medalist, *First Snow* by Nancy Viau (Albert Whitman, 2018); and *On Your Way* written by John Coy and published by Beaming Books. *Finding Beauty* is Talitha's first author/illustrator adventure.